THE GIFT OF CHANGING WOMAN

by Tryntje Van Ness Seymour

Henry Holt and Company ◆ New York

This book is dedicated
to Apache medicine man Philip Cassadore,
who understood the importance
of preserving cultural traditions and values
while at the same time respecting those
of cultures different from one's own.
With humility he listened
to the voices of the Mountain Spirits,
and with courage he found his voice
to share what he believed in with others.

Henry Holt and Company, Inc.
Publishers since 1866
115 West 18th Street
New York, New York 10011

Henry Holt is a registered trademark of Henry Holt and Company, Inc.

Library of Congress Cataloging-in-Publication Data
Seymour, Tryntje Van Ness.
The gift of Changing Woman / by Tryntje Van Ness Seymour.
p.   cm.
Includes bibliographical references.
Summary: Describes the traditional coming-of-age ceremony for young Apache women, in which they use special dances and prayers
to reenact the Apache story of creation and celebrate the power of Changing Woman, the legendary ancestor of their people.
1. Apache Indians—Legends.   2. Apache Indians—Women—Juvenile literature. 3. Apache Indians—Rites and ceremonies—Juvenile literature.
[1. Apache Indians—Rites and ceremonies.   2. Apache Indians—Legends. 3. Indians of North America—Rites and ceremonies.
4. Indians of North America—Legends.]   I. Title.   E99.A6S48   1993   299′.74—dc20   92-31833

ISBN 0-8050-2577-4

First Edition—1993

Printed in the United States of America on acid-free paper. ∞

1 3 5 7 9 10 8 6 4 2

Map by Robert Romagnoli

ABOUT THIS BOOK

City subways, skyscrapers, and crowds at rush hour were what I grew up with— and they were a long way away that night I stood in a crowded circle of celebrants at an Apache Changing Woman ceremony in Arizona. Rugged hills and mountains surrounded us, not pavement and high rises. And there were no street lights, only the light from the moon and the fire.

Listening to the people cheer as the ceremony went on through the night, I knew how important this was to them, and I wanted to know why.

Apache medicine man Philip Cassadore, perhaps the leading authority on the Changing Woman ceremony, invited me to attend the ceremony and to visit his family's home so that I could get to know his people better. I did. That night and in later visits and conversations I learned about the Mountain Spirits and the Gift of Changing Woman. And I learned about values the Apache have cherished for generations. What I learned has enriched my life.

This book grew out of those visits. Philip Cassadore, who taught me most about the Apache, was concerned about the well-being of his people, and he urged me to share what I learned with others so that they too might better understand, appreciate, and respect the Apache people and their way of life.

Throughout this book Cassadore's words, as well as those of his sister Pansy Cassadore and artist Delmar Boni, tell us more about the ceremony and the Apache way. Their words appear in italics. I have saved identifying the individual speakers until page 34. When you read their words, try to hear, as I do, the people speaking in their own voices.

In order to convey a sense of the ceremony as the Apache people see it themselves, all of the images in the book are paintings by Apache artists. Using only Apache art allows us to see the ceremony and the Mountain Spirits through Apache eyes, not through the eyes of outsiders.

Information about the people quoted, the artists of the paintings and the paintings themselves, will be found in the Author's Note at the end of the book.

Along time ago, the Apache story goes, there was a terrible flood. Water covered the land and all living things.

Only one person, Changing Woman, managed to survive, which she did by sealing herself inside an abalone shell. After the waters shrank back, she climbed out of the shell and wandered around the empty land, leaving places of beauty in her trail, places such as those now known as Monument Valley and the San Francisco Peaks.

Changing Woman came to live in Oak Creek Canyon, a glen of red-rock walls, lush trees and plants, and a sparkling stream. Although it was beautiful, she was lonely, for she was the only person left alive, and there were no birds, nor any other living creatures.

One day she heard a voice.

The voice said, "Go over there and kneel down when the sun comes up." So she did this, three times—she kneeled every morning for three days—and nothing happened. Then she said to herself, Well, nothing happened, so I'm not going to do that again. The voice came to her again and said, "Do it a fourth time." She did it a fourth time, and she became pregnant [by the sun] and bore a son.

Then she was told, the same way with the water, "Go down to where the water is dripping," and again she tried three times and became discouraged. But she was told to try again, and the fourth time she became pregnant [by the water] and bore a son.

And those three people, Changing Woman and her two sons, were the first people, from whom we all came.

As descendants of Changing Woman, the Apache people cherish the land she lived in, and they revere Changing Woman as the first mother of the people. She represents the ideal woman.

Women play an important role in Apache society. The Apache belong to various clans, or extended families, and children join their mother's clan, not their father's.

This goes back to the Apache creation story of Changing Woman and her two sons, one by the sun and one by the water. The mother is the earth, the father is the sun. In Apache we say you lean toward the father, but you are with the mother. You lean toward the sun, but it is in the sky, distant. You touch the earth and are close to it, part of it. So, you are a member of your mother's clan.

When an Apache girl comes of age, at about twelve or thirteen years old, she stands on the verge of her own womanhood. The people have a ceremony to help her in this transition, to prepare her for life as a woman. In the ceremony they call the power of Changing Woman to the girl. The story of Changing Woman is retold and reenacted, and through the ceremony the girl receives blessings, guidance, advice, and an example of how she should live her life. As the Apache see it, during the ceremony she goes from girlhood to womanhood. There is no "adolescence" in Apache life.

Apache parents will tell their daughter, "This ceremony is what I want you to have, because I want you to have a good life, a long life, ahead of you." And a girl feels honored to accept that.

My mom and dad wanted me to have this ceremony. They told me that I would have a blessing and a good life. And they told me, "After you have this dance, you're not a child anymore. You must put away all your playthings." And I thought, How can this be? I'm still young. But that's how you feel after the dance is over. You're not a child anymore.

In Apache the ceremony is called *Na'íí'ees,* which means that the ceremony is happening and the people are getting the girl ready for womanhood. In English the ceremony is known as the Gift of Changing Woman. Some call it the Sunrise Ceremony.

The ceremony is a major undertaking on the part of the girl's family, her godparents' family, and her community. It requires months of preparation and a great deal of hard work and expense. Godparents serve as the girl's sponsors for the ceremony, and they will remain close to the girl for the rest of her life. When the girl's family chooses godparents, they look for a godmother whose good reputation commands respect in the community, someone who can be a good role model for the girl.

The *Na'íí'ees* ceremony lasts four days, and is usually held in summer when the weather is best and people are free to attend. It takes place out in the open country, with a large, flat area for dancing, plus space for cooking and feasting and setting up the camps of the immediate families and the hundreds of attending clan members and friends.

The first two days of the ceremony are private. The second two are public, shared and participated in by as many friends and relatives as possible. They are there to lend their prayers and support to the girl, and in the process, by joining together and reaffirming the Apache way of life, they are themselves strengthened.

At dawn on the third day of the ceremony the girl and her godmother stand together in the center of the dance area, facing the sunrise.

For the girl, this is a day to feel proud and mature as she sees hundreds of relatives and friends gathering in a giant circle of well-wishers around her. On her shoulders she can feel the weight of her specially made outfit: a soft yellow buckskin top, with fringe and tin cone tinklers that hang down over a colorful tiered cloth skirt, and a beaded neckpiece encircling her neck and hanging over the buckskin on her shoulders and chest. In her hair, at the back of her head, dangles a white feather. A piece of abalone shell is tied to her hair and hangs over her forehead. On her feet she wears high-topped moccasins.

She holds a yellow cane, attached to which are small, round bells, eagle feathers, a piece of turquoise, and fluttering streamers of ribbon.

The girl and her godmother stand with dignity as they dance in place with a fast shuffling step to the sound of chanting that comes from behind them. Close to her ear the girl can hear the words of the medicine man, who serves as a religious leader and spiritual guide to his people. Today he conducts the girl's ceremony, and for much of this day he will sing the chants of Changing Woman, telling the story of creation, accompanied by a chorus of men and four drums that beat a rhythm to the chants.

With each beat of the drums the girl pounds her cane on the ground, making the bells on the cane jingle. The fringe on her heavy dress responds to every move she makes, and the dangling tin pieces tinkle and clink.

The songs and everything in the ceremony tell the creation story of the earth. The girl goes through the creation story. She has to listen to the songs. She has to really concentrate on them while she is dancing. She is not just dancing there; she has to listen.

While she dances, the girl concentrates on the meaning of the songs and pays close attention to everything she does. During earlier parts of the ceremony, and even before the ceremony began, the girl's mother, her godmother, the medicine man, and other elders gave her instructions about what was coming and how she should behave. They told her that the songs would be important and that her dance movements would reflect the meaning of the songs. The songs and the actions of the ceremony take the girl through the creation story. And, at the same time, everything that happens in the ceremony is related to her future life as a woman, and is meant to bring her blessings and good fortune and long life.

She can see this prayer for long life in the cane she holds. The cane stands for old age. When she gets old, she may need the cane to help her walk. The white feather in her hair represents the prayer that she will live to the age of white hair. The abalone shell on her forehead associates her with the power of White Shell Woman (another name for Changing Woman, who hid from the flood inside an abalone shell).

The sun creeps up the sky, and the girl and her godmother continue to dance. When the sun is well above the horizon, the girl kneels, and, with elbows bent, hands by her shoulders, palms facing forward, she sways back and forth, looking towards the sun. She reenacts the position Changing Woman took when she became pregnant.

A little later in the morning, the girl leans forward onto a soft pile of blankets topped with a deer hide that sits on the ground before her. Now she represents Changing Woman's children. She stretches out full length, face down, and lies still, like a lump of clay. Then she lets her godmother move around her, massaging her from head to toe. The older woman molds the girl as if she were a baby: she touches her eyes, to make them open, and her mouth. The godmother is "molding" her because Changing Woman's children at first were clay, which she had to mold into shape, forming their bodies. This massage is also meant to give the girl good posture and form.

After the massage the girl stands up and resumes her dancing. As the sun climbs high, the day grows hot and the air dry and still. She dances on, knowing she must not give in to fatigue. She must be strong.

Some of the men and women in the surrounding circle of family and friends link arms and join in the dancing. The women wear long, gathered skirts and loose tops, what they call camp dresses, in a rainbow of vibrant colors. In their lines the dancers move slowly in towards the girl and then out towards the outer circle.

They have to be there to support her. In all this dancing, it's all praying. The family and friends are right behind the girl with prayers. The ladies and men dancing don't talk to each other, because in their hearts they are praying—for her and all the people and all the world. Their prayers are for her, but also for things that are important to all Apache: the plants, the rain, the mountains; just about everything on this earth.

Late in the morning, the girl hands her beribboned cane to someone who takes it away to the east of her and plants it firmly in the ground. Then, her hair streaming out behind her and her buckskin fringe flapping wildly, the girl runs, as fast as she can, out and around the cane. Many of her family and friends follow close on her heels. They do this four times, with the cane placed farther away from her each time. The four runs represent the stages of life, from infancy to childhood to adulthood to old age, and she runs fast to ensure that she will be healthy all her life and live long.

By now the sun is high overhead. At midday, while the girl continues dancing, her family and friends line up in front of her and, one by one, each person says a prayer and sprinkles a handful of yellow pollen over her head, chest, and shoulders. This is their way of blessing her. She receives these blessings with quiet dignity as scores of people offer their prayers in turn, and soon her hair and face are yellow with pollen. In the extreme heat someone fans her with a hat.

It's hard to dance four days, but you have to. You just keep thinking, Can I make it? Can I dance the four days, dancing night and day? At the beginning you ask yourself, Will I make it?

When it's over, you feel so relieved. And people pray for you, putting the pollen on you. And with all that energy and strength and the prayers they said for you, you feel blessed. I guess it makes a person stronger.

When everyone who wishes to has blessed the girl, the morning's dance is almost over. Then the girl removes each blanket from the pile she lay on earlier, shakes it, and throws it—one to each of the four directions, to ensure a clean home and plenty of blankets. And then she retires to her own camp for more counsel with the elders.

Tonight the *Gaan* will come.

The Apache people—the descendants of Changing Woman—live today in a land of mountains: mountainous desert with cacti, mountain foothills with juniper and scrub, mountain uplands with pines and snow. A wide-ranging, tough terrain, Apache land reaches across millions of acres in what is now eastern Arizona, with two smaller areas in northern and southeastern New Mexico.

Although beautiful, the land is hard and demanding. For those who can listen to the land, however, it can be rich and fruitful.

We can see a mountain, in a real simple way, as something beautiful: the colors change in the evening, it gives out life at a certain time of year, and when certain seasons come, life goes on. But that is not the end. Just as we see with the crescent moon: the crescent moon is not the ending, it is another beginning. It perpetuates that message, that life goes on. . . .

It's the same with the mountain. It bears yucca or it bears the pine or these various things that we need, that are essential to us. We know that when their harvest is gone, that is not the end of it. Because the rain will come over again, over that mountain; the lightning will bless it; the water will fall on the seedling. It will start growing again, growing toward the light, that light that comes with the day.

When the sky brightens at dawn each morning and the sun pours its first light across the mountains of Apache land, traditional Apache people start their day by facing the sun and saying a prayer. Showing respect for the forces of nature is at the heart of the Apache way of life. The mountains, and the hardships the people face, have taught the Apache to respect the natural world around them.

Living in a land of mountains and hardship, the Apache people cherish especially the power they know as the Mountain Spirits. Called *Gaan,* the powerful and benevolent Mountain Spirits share their friendship and protection with the Apache.

The story of the Mountain Spirits goes back to the earliest days of the earth, back to the time of creation.

It started in the east. . . . It was all black, black, before the earth was made. Everything was black. The creation started from there. . . . It all came from there. It came from black.

In Apache, the color black is always associated with the east, where creation began.

Out of the blackness, the earth was created. And then the sky was made blue, giving the color blue to the south. Then the sun was made, bringing the color yellow to the west. And then came the white clouds and the thunder, and the color white became the color of the north.

When the earth was created, it needed something to hold it steady. And so a *Gaan*—a benevolent spirit—was made to hold the earth. He stood in the east and supported the earth, like a table leg holding a table. But the earth would not stand still. It wobbled.

So another leg [in the form of a Gaan] was made to stand in the south. And the earth still wobbled. Then they made another leg, to stand in the west. And the earth still wobbled a bit. Until they made one more leg, standing in the north. And the earth stood still. So that is how the earth was created on the fourth day, and these are the people who did it.

With the foundation of the earth resting on them, steady and secure, the four *Gaan* represent balance and stability. At one time the *Gaan* lived as people. But then they left the surface world to live within the mountains. And now they live eternally in spirit form. They are sacred. They protect the people, and the land and the animals, and they can help to heal the sick and the ailing.

Sometimes the Apache people call on the Mountain Spirits to lend their power to a ceremony. The Mountain Spirits join in ceremonies by appearing in the physical form of specially clothed men who imitate the *Gaan* and dance in their special way. They are accompanied by a medicine man, who knows the songs of the Mountain Spirits, and he sings while they dance.

Everything about the *Gaan*—from the symbols depicted on them and what they represent, to the sounds they make—is related to nature and the powers of the world.

With bodies painted black– the color of the east, where the creation of the world began— the *Gaan* traditionally wear yellow buckskin kilts with belts. The kilts have fringe along the bottom, sometimes with shell or tin cone tinklers that make a clinking sound as they move. Rain is precious to the Apache, and the sound of the tinklers represents the sound of rain hitting the sun-dried hard ground during a rainstorm. In each hand the dancers carry a wooden wand that is painted with a zigzag line signifying the power of lightning, a good power, associated with rain. Long fluttering ribbons, which jerk and move during the dance, also depict lightning. And the *Gaan* make a sound with their voices that is said to be like thunder.

The colors and designs painted on the crowns and bodies of the dancers have special meaning. Rounded shapes portray the earth or the sun or the moon. The image of the crescent moon suggests natural cycles, like the phases of the moon. The colors black, blue, yellow, and white represent the cardinal directions. Yellow also refers to the sun. White stands for clouds as well as the north. The cross shape and the four-pointed star also symbolize the four directions, implying the entire universe.

Because there are four Mountain Spirits, the *Gaan* dancers appear as a group of four. The number four is sacred in the Apache way. It reflects the four directions and is associated with balance and harmony, central values to the Apache way of life. To be in harmony with the powers of the universe is the Apache ideal.

These dancers are a strong mesenger of the lifeway, of how people see themselves in balance with the earth.

The four *Gaan* dancers are generally accompanied by a fifth figure, called *Łibaiyé*, the Gray One. He is gray because he represents the whirlwind, which looks gray as it spins dust and sand into a twisting spiral of air. A design representing a bear track is often painted on his chest or back, so that the Gray One can rid the people of evil—because some Apache believe that bears are the reincarnation of evil people.

The Gray One usually carries a bullroarer in his right hand. The bullroarer is a flat piece of wood attached to an arm's-length piece of string. When the bullroarer is swung around in a circle, the piece of wood spins at the end of the string and makes a whirring sound, like the sound of the wind.

Sometimes the Gray One also speaks a soft sound: *"ooOOOOoooooo"*—the voice of the wind. To the Apache, he is the whirlwind; he is the wind. Without the whirlwind, they say, the people don't breathe; there is no air.

And so the *Gaan* and *Łibaiyé* come together. The Mountain Spirits—the *Gaan*—are predictable, stable. The foundation of the world rests on them. The Gray One is unpredictable. He represents the element of chance that comes into a person's life. With the predictable and unpredictable together there is equilibrium, balance.

One needs to have strength, balance, to face the unpredictable in life—this is one of the key understandings the Apache people draw from the appearance of the *Gaan* and *Łibaiyé*.

When night falls on the third day of the Changing Woman ceremony, the people build a bonfire and set it ablaze. Happy and excited, hundreds of friends and relatives of the girl pack together in a large and crowded semicircle around the fire.

The four *Gaan* and *Łibaiyé,* the Gray One, come and stand in a line opposite the semicircle, completing the circle around the fire. The girl being honored in the ceremony stands between the first Mountain Spirit and the next. Following each of the Mountain Spirits stands another girl— four in all, who are given the honor of joining the girl tonight because they will be the next to have their own ceremony. All the girls wear beautiful buckskin outfits. The girls and the Mountain Spirits move restlessly, ready to begin; their dangling bells and tinklers chatter.

Everyone waits, the air charged with excitement. The moon hangs above, quiet, remote, giving a gentle light to the late night. The nearby mountains stand close and friendly.

A single loud and deep-voiced drum begins to beat. The chorus begins to sing: loud, strong, fast.

And then the *Gaan* dance, jumping and swinging in the air. Forming a line, they zigzag in towards the fire, then out towards the crowd. Twisting and bending their bodies, the *Gaan* throw their crowned heads forward and down and then jerk them up, lifting and thrusting their arms and wands into the air. The girl and her companions dance with them, following their movements. The Gray One twirls his bullroarer, making the sound of rushing, stormy wind and thunder.

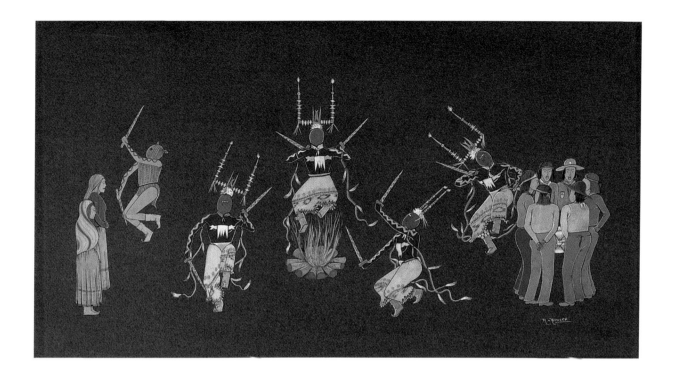

The Gaan come because they have a good spirit. So they are part of it. They help purify the girl. They make her strong with their spirit.

This is close to the end of the ceremony, the last night. It means that we are making a joyful noise, we are making a joyful sound.

The crowd responds, celebrating, shouting, cheering, crowding closer, singing, dancing. Lines of men and women dance along the inside edge of the circle. They move in time with the song and the drum. The fire itself seems to dance, sending up showers of sparks to the moon.

At dawn the following morning, after a brief rest, the people gather again. The sun sits low on the horizon, making long shadows. The light shines clean and gentle in the cool air.

Facing the rising sun, the girl dances once more, knowing that this will be the last day of her long ceremony. Today she will complete her transformation, and she will be painted with the clay of White Painted Lady (a third name for Changing Woman and White Shell Woman). She stands in the center of a framework of four poles, which represents the home of White Painted Lady. The poles are slender young trees that have been stripped bare except for the tender leafy branches at the tops above where the poles meet and are tied together, and the clusters of leaves shiver in the morning breeze. As before, while she dances, a large chorus sings with the medicine man, accompanied by four drums.

(Gilbert Cosen)

As the people come together again to stand in a large circle around the dance area, *Łibaiyé* runs in from the east and begins to dance in honor of the girl, whipping around and spinning his bull-roarer. He is followed by the *Gaan,* who jump, and run, and move back and forth and around, tilting this way and that, jerking their heads down and to the side, making dramatic movements with their headpieces while they twist and jab with their wands.

As suddenly as they came, the *Gaan* return to the east, leaving behind a deep silence, which contrasts with the noise and action of their dance.

The girl continues to dance quietly, with her godfather dancing beside her now. Off to one side sits a large basket, and, out of the corner of her eye, the girl can see someone pouring water into it and then mixing in it the paint that will be used to complete her transformation into White Painted Lady.

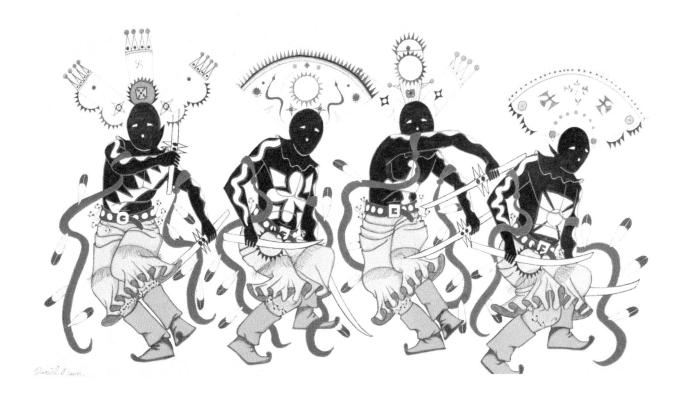

All around her she sees and feels the support of her community: her family and friends offering their prayers for her health and happiness while they dance in the crowded circle that surrounds her, the medicine man and the chorus singing behind her, her godparents working to make the ceremony a success.

The *Gaan* return, and the crowd moves in closer to her. A long, loose brush made of plant stems sits in the basket of paint. The first *Gaan* walks up to the basket and dips the brush into the paint. Then he takes the loaded brush, and the girl can feel the fine liquid clay drip down her face and hair as he gently paints it on her, blessing her with it. Each of the *Gaan* in turn drapes the paint over her as if it were a shawl, covering her from the top of her head down.

Soon the paint lies thickly on the girl, caked on her face and buckskin dress, sticking to her like mud.

The paint is not pure white but a grayish-white color. It is a special paint.

That is their paint. The Mountain Spirits brought it with them from another world. The paint they use is made up of four different colors of the earth. Like the colors of the Painted Desert.

They go out and hunt yellow paint, and they put it in there. They have a stone that is blue; they grind it and put that in there. And there is black and there is white. And they mix it all together and paint her with that.

A long time ago the earth was a kind of grayish color, because, I guess, it was mostly water. That is the way the Apache tell the story. The earth had more water than it does now. There was water all over. Then later there became some land— a little place here, a little place there, a little place there—where people can live. And the earth was kind of gray. That is how they knew the gray color to paint the girl with.

The *Gaan* keep dancing and moving close around her. The women and some of the men dance alongside. Now it is happening. The girl is becoming a woman.

Mustering all her strength for the long and strenuous *Na'ii'ees* ceremony, the girl proves she can handle the demands placed on her, and she comes to understand both the hardship and the promise of adult Apache life. She learns that she will be expected to work hard, with no more time for the play of childhood, but with that work will come blessings, among them the blessings of her association with Changing Woman and her joining the adult community and the joy of being able to raise her own children.

After the ceremony you feel proud, because you made it through those four days. You think to yourself, I'm a woman now. I'm not a child anymore. And you start thinking about your future; you're looking forward to it.

The large circle of friends and family tightens together, becoming a smaller circle, closing around her as if in one huge embrace. Finally transformed into White Painted Lady, she takes the basket of paint, cradling it with both arms, and turns to slowly walk around the inside edge of the circle. The medicine man and the *Gaan* accompany her, and her godfather walks beside her. As they walk, she carries the basket at chest height, and her godfather takes the brush and dips it into the paint, then gracefully swings the loaded brush up and out, so that the paint arcs out through the air and spatters the crowd, sharing the blessings of Changing Woman—White Painted Lady—with all the people.

After completing a stately and solemn tour of the circle of people, the procession, now including the chorus, moves through the four-sided pole structure once in each direction. Joining the procession, the people in the crowd follow, their faces and clothes flecked with the paint of White Painted Lady.

They march in four different directions. Then everything is good: The girl has gone through this, and we called these people and we called those, and we called all the spirits of all kinds; we had four or five medicine men all around the girl, and there will be a happy road for her, wherever she goes, however long she lives on this earth.

One last time the people gather in a circle, this time standing around the ashes of last night's bonfire. Two men take turns addressing the crowd, thanking the people and saying it has been good. Then the *Gaan* dance four more times around the ashes, touching their wands to the ashes.

Clouds of dust, raised from the dry earth by many feet, make the air thick. The dust seems to mingle with the dance of the *Gaan* and the people. The songs and the bells and the movement and the color vibrate to the rhythm of the drum.

Then you just dance, like shaking it off. You dance. And all the disease and all the bad thinking comes off you.

White Painted Lady, for the girl is now White Painted Lady, or Changing Woman, stands with her godmother on the inside edge of the circle of people, joined now with the others. She has been blessed. She has been welcomed to the adult community. Today she is a woman. And, as she stands there at the edge of the circle, she foreshadows her future self as an old lady: her face wrinkled with clay and her hair gray. She leans, world weary, with arms crossed, on her cane.

From this day on she will be treated as a woman and expected to act with good harmony and to set a good example. For the girl, the ceremony has been a test of her endurance as well as an honor and a blessing. It has been both a symbolic preparation for her adult responsibilities and a real one. She has learned from the advice of her elders, from the example of her godmother, and from the story of Changing Woman. She has been blessed by the Mountain Spirits. She has gained a deep inner strength. Most important, perhaps, after benefiting from the support of her family, friends, and community throughout the ceremony, she has come to understand that the greatest strength of the Apache way of life is the people's commitment to one another.

That's how I found out, when I had my dance. I think that was given to us from the beginning of the world, from creation; it was given to us, and it just keeps coming down—commitment to each other.

The ceremony for the girl has also been for the people: Retelling the story of creation. Bringing the power of Changing Woman and its blessings. Reinforcing basic values. Everyone comes together. People give of themselves to the ceremony, and, as the girl becomes a woman, changing before their eyes, it happens for everyone. For the Apache people, tradition and history prepare the way for the future in the land of mountains and Mountain Spirits.

> *We struggle, and we go through these canyons, we go through these mountains, and we find some central things: the goodness of mankind, to be a part of the earth, to have an understanding that we are caretakers of the earth for this period that we are here as people. . . . Be good to these things that are around us—the trees, the animals, the eagles, the deer, the water, the sky; simple things, these simple things that are quite near to us.*
>
> *And, as we perpetuate that message, generation to generation of young Apache people stand on the earth and watch that sun come over the horizon.*

The *Gaan* finish their dance. White Painted Lady runs in a circle around the ashes; then she and the Mountain Spirits run off to the east, leaving the dance area behind.

The ceremony is over.
The poles are taken down.
The Mountain Spirits return to the mountains.
The people go to feast.

AUTHOR'S NOTE

When the Spaniards and then the Anglos came to Apache land, many Apache traditions changed. Today, instead of hunting animals and gathering wild plants for their living, the Apache raise cattle, cut lumber, work in offices, and help tourists. The Apache used to move from place to place and live in temporary camps of dome-shaped brush shelters called *gowa,* which smelled sweetly of fresh-cut boughs. Now the Apache live in modern houses and towns and wear blue jeans and T-shirts and other Anglo-style clothing. Apache children go to public schools, and the people speak English as well as their own language.

But some things have not changed. The Apache still live on their land, and many still listen to the old stories and draw their strength from the mountains. The Gift of Changing Woman is still very much a part of the Apache way of life.

The information in this book is based primarily on the author's interviews with Apache people, some of whose quotes are used in the text (as well as on less formal conversations with other Apache people, and general research). Obviously, the result reflects the personal views of these individuals, which may vary from the views of others. Like Christians, Jews, and people of other faiths, Apache people differ in their beliefs from one person to the next. This book does not describe everyone's experience. The Apache people are not stuck in some sort of time warp—these are modern people living in the present day who make their own choices.

It is not easy for a non-Indian to communicate information and ideas about Native American people, their ceremonies, and their beliefs. One must be extremely sensitive to rights of privacy and matters of religious belief and practices that are not to be shared with outsiders. This sensitivity and a respectful attitude were not only a part of the process of researching and writing this book, but are also in themselves goals of the book.

Language can be a limitation in communicating about one culture to another. The English word "dance" has become accepted in describing Native American religious ceremonies, but the term can be misleading. These are not dances for entertainment but rather body movement that contributes to the expression of prayer. The dances are part of the practice of religion and are sacred.

The terms "godmother" and "godparents" can also be confusing. As well as serving in their formal roles during the girl's ceremony, the sponsors help bear the cost and help organize the ceremony. Serving as a sponsor is demanding, but it is also an honor. Although not exactly the same as Christian godparents, the sponsors of a *Na'íí'ees* ceremony serve in a similar capacity—offering guidance, support, and advice—and so the use of these English words to refer to the sponsors has become common.

Another language problem lies within the use of the word "Apache." While historically, and still today, non-Indians use this word to refer to these people, they call themselves *Ndee* (meaning "the people") in their own language. To avoid confusion, the word Apache has been used in this book, but it would be useful, whenever seeing the word Apache, to think of what they call themselves—the people.

THE SPEAKERS

Most of the quotes in this book are the words of Philip Cassadore, San Carlos Apache medicine man, who conducted the *Na'íí'ees* ceremony many times and served as a spiritual leader. His words appear on pages 7, 8 (top), 11, 16, 17, 24, 28, 30, and 31 (top). Cassadore dedicated much of his life to trying to bridge the gap between cultures, as well as guiding people in the Apache way and helping the traditional ways to continue, including playing a key role in carrying on the *Na'íí'ees* ceremony. As one of his efforts to bring people together with mutual respect, he conducted a weekly Apache-language radio broadcast of world events.

The quotes on pages 15, 20, and 32 are from Delmar Boni, a San Carlos Apache artist and father of several young children. Early in his career Boni was inspired by the art of Allan Houser and other Apache painters whose works are included here, and he is also inspired by the mountains and the Mountain Spirits, which have been central figures in his own artwork.

The quotes on pages 8 (bottom), 13, 14, 29, and 31 (bottom) are from Pansy Cassadore, a San Carlos Apache woman whose mother held a *Na'íí'ees* ceremony for her when she came of age, and who has participated in many ceremonies for other girls. She is Philip Cassadore's sister.

The description of *Na'íí'ees*, the Changing Woman Ceremony, partly reflects a ceremony attended by the author in September 1984 near San Carlos, Arizona. Attending the ceremony was at the invitation of Philip Cassadore, and he and his family were gracious hosts during that visit. Cassadore consulted with the author on several occasions and served as guide and teacher in the Apache way. Cassadore has since traveled on to the next world, but his words are used here in the present tense to record them in the spirit in which he first gave them.

THE ARTISTS

The paintings used to illustrate this book are all works by Apache artists and are all from museum collections throughout the United States. Some of the artists pursued careers with their artwork, while others painted for only a short while. Information about the artists is given here in roughly chronological order by birth date.

Naiche (sometimes spelled Nachee) achieved renown as the Chiricahua Apache leader who, alongside Geronimo, evaded federal troops during the mid-1880s. Naiche and Geronimo, and their small band of warriors, finally surrendered to General Nelson Miles and his force of five thousand troops in 1886, when the Apache leaders were promised favorable conditions for themselves and their people. Instead of being allowed to return to their homeland as promised, however, the Chiricahua Apache were sent to imprisonment in Fort Marion, Florida, and later moved to Fort Sill, Oklahoma. During his imprisonment, Naiche became known for his artwork. He painted at least two deerskins with images of the *Na'íí'ees* ceremony, perhaps out of concern that the ceremony might someday be lost.

Born on February 17, 1902, near Fort Sill, Oklahoma, Moses Loco spent the first twelve years of his life as a prisoner of war, along with his parents and the other Chiricahua Apache. He never studied art, and he painted mostly for his own pleasure. Occasionally he exhibited his work at local county fairs and won awards. He died in April 1990.

Allan Houser is the most widely recognized Apache artist. Famous throughout the world for his sculpture, a piece of which was commissioned to stand in front of the United Nations building in New York City, Houser began his art career as a painter—although one could say he actually began when he was a little boy and played with clay along creek banks. A Chiricahua Apache, Houser was born near Fort Sill, Oklahoma, in 1914, just after the Chiricahua had been released from twenty-five years of imprisonment. While growing up, he sketched at home, where his mother did beadwork and his father told stories of the old days and sang traditional songs. Houser studied painting under Dorothy Dunn at The Studio in Santa Fe, and went on to paint and do murals. He was encouraged by a later teacher to take up sculpture, and for many years he painted and sculpted in his free time while teaching art for a living. Now that he is no longer teaching, he spends most of his time sculpting in the studio he built for himself south of Santa Fe. He has exhibited extensively and won numerous awards and honors, among them a Guggenheim fellowship and the French *Palmes d'Académiques*. In July 1992 he was the first Native American to receive the United States' highest award, the National Medal of Art. A retrospective of his career filled galleries at two museums in Santa Fe in 1991, and his life and art have been the subject of many articles and a lengthy book.

Wilson Dewey was born June 25, 1915, in old San Carlos. After early schooling near San Carlos, he attended the Santa Fe Indian School from 1935 to 1938 and graduated from high school at the Albuquerque Indian School. He served in the U.S. Army during World War II and later lived and worked as an artist—and calf roper—in Santa Fe. His artwork has been published a number of times and exhibited widely. He once said of his painting, "What I like to paint best are animals and Apache Crown Dancers [*Gaan*]. I am a full-blooded Apache Indian from San Carlos—I am very proud of my tribe and to be one of them." He died in January 1969.

Ignatius Palmer began receiving attention for his artwork in grade school, when he won several prizes. A Mescalero Apache, Palmer was born in 1921. He attended The Studio at the Santa Fe Indian School, where he studied with San Juan Pueblo artist and teacher Geronima Cruz Montoya, and where he sold his first painting. He served in the Army Air Corps for three years in Europe during World War II and, out of homesickness, developed an even deeper appreciation for Mescalero Apache land. He worked in building construction for a number of years but also continued to paint, and after returning home to Mescalero he exhibited his work mostly in the Mescalero area. He designed the Mescalero Apache tribe logo, and his favorite subject was the Mountain Spirit Dancers. "I try to paint the real Mescalero," he said. "The Mescalero I knew."

Mescalero Apache artist Rudolph Treas attended the Santa Fe Indian School and later studied art at the University of Arizona. He exhibited his work from the late 1940s through the early 1960s and won awards from the School of American Research, the Museum of New Mexico, and the Philbrook Art Center. He died in August 1969.

Roger Dickson lived in San Carlos, Arizona. Little is known about his work. The painting that appears in this book is from the collection of Dorothy Dunn, who created The Studio, an art program at the Santa Fe Indian School. Written on the back of the painting is a note that says the painting was purchased at The Shop in Santa Fe in 1965.

Not much is known, either, about Daniel Nash. Born in San Carlos, Arizona, he moved to New Mexico and attended high school on the Mescalero Apache reservation. He later lived in Texas.

Gilbert Cosen, of Whiteriver, Arizona, was born at home on August 23, 1941, in the small community of Canyon Day. He remembers being interested in painting as a child of six or seven. He attended boarding schools on the White Mountain reservation in Arizona, and then went to Bacone College from 1960 to 1961, where he was a student of well-known artist Dick West. He praises Dick West for his masterful teaching and encouragement. While at college Cosen sold paintings and entered his work in exhibitions at the Philbrook Art Center. Cosen received a scholarship to attend the Southwest Indian Art Project at the University of Arizona in 1962. Then he returned home to the White Mountains and made a career of working in the forestry department of the Bureau of Indian Affairs, occasionally painting throughout the years for family and friends.

More extensive biographical information about some of these artists (Allan Houser, Wilson Dewey, and Ignatius Palmer) and further details about their work and the Apache way of life can be found in the author's longer work, *When the Rainbow Touches Down: The Artists and Stories Behind the Apache, Navajo, Rio Grande Pueblo and Hopi Paintings in the William and Leslie Van Ness Denman Collection* (published by The Heard Museum, Phoenix, Arizona, 1989). One of the chapters in that book provided source material for this one.

THE PAINTINGS

The paintings are listed here in the order in which they appear in the book. The list includes the page number on which the painting appears, the name of the artist, the museum's title of the work (if there is one), the date of the painting, the medium, the dimensions (height precedes width), and the name of the institution that owns the work, along with its catalog number. In some cases, details from the paintings are used as well as the full paintings. Where this is the case, the page or pages on which these details appear are noted in parentheses following the entry for the painting.

page 11. Allan Houser. *Apache Girls' Adolescent Ceremony.* 1938. Opaque watercolor on paper. 12 × 18½ inches. Museum of Northern Arizona, catalog no. C153, accession no. 1355. (Details on 8 and 10.)

page 18. Wilson Dewey. *Gaan and Łibaiyé (Mountain Spirits and the Gray One).* 1937. Tempera on cream-colored paper. 21½ × 29¾ inches. U.S. Department of the Interior, Indian Arts and Crafts Board, William and Leslie Van Ness Denman Collection, no. W-68.56.266. (Details on 16 and 17.)

page 19, left. Ignatius Palmer. *Gaan (Mountain Spirit).* 1938. Casein on paper. 11½ × 9 inches. U.S. Department of the Interior, Indian Arts and Crafts Board, William and Leslie Van Ness Denman Collection, no. W-68.56.270.

page 19, right. Ignatius Palmer. *Gaan (Mountain Spirit).* ca. 1939. Casein on illustration board. 7¼ × 4¾ inches. U.S. Department of the Interior, Indian Arts and Crafts Board, William and Leslie Van Ness Denman Collection, no. W-68.56.271.

page 20. Allan Houser. *Gaan (Mountain Spirit).* 1936. Casein on paper. 13½ × 10½ inches. U.S. Department of the Interior, Indian Arts and Crafts Board, William and Leslie Van Ness Denman Collection, no. W-68.56.267.

page 21. Anonymous. *Łibaiyé (The Gray One).* ca. 1930–1935. Tempera on buff-colored paper. 9¾ × 7¾ inches. U.S. Department of the Interior, Indian Arts and Crafts Board, William and Leslie Van Ness Denman Collection, no. W-68.56.265.

page 22. Moses Loco. *Nighttime Apache Dance.* Date unknown. Oil. 16 × 22½ inches. Museum of Northern Arizona, catalog no. C1331, accession no. 2641.

page 24. Allan Houser. *Gaan (Mountain Spirit Dance).* ca. 1936–1938. Tempera on dark brown-colored paper. 14½ × 25⅝ inches. U.S. Department of the Interior, Indian Arts and Crafts Board, William and Leslie Van Ness Denman Collection, no. W-68.56.269.

page 25. Roger Dickson. Untitled. 1936. Gouache on paper. 29.5 × 57 centimeters. Museum of New Mexico, Laboratory of Anthropology/Museum of Indian Arts and Culture, no. 51361/13.

page 26. Gilbert Cosen. *Mountain Spirit Dancers*. 1960. Opaque watercolor on paper. 12½ × 21 inches. Museum of Northern Arizona, catalog no. C1071, accession no. 2641.

page 27. Daniel Nash. *Devil Dance (Four Mountain Spirits)*. ca 1970. Watercolor on textured cream paper. 10⅜ × 20½ inches. School of American Research, Santa Fe, New Mexico, no. SAR 1989-7-362.

page 29. Rudolph Treas. *Devil Dancers and Girls*. 1960. Opaque watercolor on paper. 13 × 16 inches. Museum of Northern Arizona, catalog no. C1153, accession no. 2641.

page 30. Allan Houser. *Apache Crown Dance*. 1952. Gouache on paper. 30 × 42 inches. Denver Art Museum, no. 1953.420. (Details on 9 and 23.)

page 39. Naiche. *Dance of the Mountain Spirits* (from the Apache Puberty Ceremony). ca. 1888–1894. Vegetable dye, ink, and pencil on deerskin. 1 × 1.23 meters. Oklahoma Historical Society, no. 3893. (Detail on 13.)

FURTHER READING

While many books have been written about the Apache, most emphasize the renowned days of warfare at the end of the nineteenth century, when the Apache were trying to defend their land and protect their way of life from the onslaught of outsiders. Unfortunately, these books are generally written from a non-Apache perspective, and therefore reading them is not an ideal way to learn about the Apache people.

The following three books consist primarily of or rely heavily on direct quotes from Apache people and for that reason make fascinating reading for people of any age and serve as a compelling introduction to Apache history and culture. They include vivid first-person accounts from older Apache individuals about traditional life. Some tell of the days of raiding and warfare in the nineteenth century. Some tell of the early days of contact with Anglos and the changes that came about. All tell about Apache life as lived by Apache people.

Ball, Eve, with Nora Henn and Linda Sanchez. *Indeh: An Apache Odyssey*. Provo, Utah: Brigham Young University Press, 1980.

Basso, Keith H., ed. *Western Apache Raiding and Warfare*. From the Notes of Grenville Goodwin. Tucson: University of Arizona Press, 1971.

Opler, Morris Edward. *An Apache Life-way: The Economic, Social and Religious Institutions of the Chiricahua Indians*. Chicago: University of Chicago Press, 1941.

The following books offer an introduction to the Apache people from the perspectives of history, ethnology, or material culture. Michael Melody's book is aimed at younger readers as well as adults.

Ferg, Alan, ed. *Western Apache Material Culture: The Goodwin and Guenther Collection.* Tucson: University of Arizona Press, 1987.

Goodwin, Grenville. *The Social Organization of the Western Apache.* Tucson: University of Arizona Press, 1969.

Mails, Thomas E. *The People Called Apache.* Englewood Cliffs, New Jersey: Prentice-Hall, 1974.

Melody, Michael E. *The Apache.* New York: Chelsea House Publishers, 1989.

Ortiz, Alfonso, ed. *Handbook of North American Indians: Southwest.* Vol. 10. William C. Sturtevant, general editor. Washington, D.C.: Smithsonian Institution, 1979.

If possible, do not learn about the Apache just by reading. Instead, try to visit Apache country and spend some time there. A major National Park Service site identified with traditional Apache land is Chiricahua National Monument, in Arizona. Apache land now known as reservations includes the San Carlos, Fort Apache, and Camp Verde reservations in Arizona, and the Jicarilla and Mescalero reservations in New Mexico.

GLOSSARY OF APACHE WORDS

Within the Apache nation there are several large divisions of people who have slightly different modes of expression and dialects. Today these divisions include the Western Apache, Chiricahua, Mescalero, Jicarilla, Lipan, and Kiowa-Apache. Included in the Western Apache are the San Carlos, White Mountain, Cibecue, and Tonto groups. This book focuses primarily on the Western Apache.

While the Apache have a strong oral tradition, words were not recorded in written form until recently when linguists, tribal members, and others worked to develop appropriate spellings. Dr. Elizabeth Brandt, linguist and associate professor of anthropology at Arizona State University, Dr. Philip Greenfeld, professor of anthropology at San Diego University, and Euella Thompson, San Carlos Apache, were consulted about the spelling and pronunciation of Apache words used here, and the words conform to the White Mountain Apache dialect and spelling, which is one of the Western Apache dialects.

About pronunciation: Each Apache word is followed in parentheses by an approximate pronunciation using letters as they would normally be pronounced in English (for example, the double *ee* is pronounced as in the English word *see,* and the *es* is pronounced as in the English word *yes*). Syllables are separated by a space, and stressed syllables are written in capital letters.

Gaan (Gahn) The Mountain Spirits; also the Mountain Spirit Dancers

gowa (go-wah) Traditional home made of willow branches

Łibaiyé (Thlee-buy-YEH) The Gray One, who accompanies the Mountain Spirit Dancers (the word literally refers to the color gray)

Na'íí'ees (Nah-ee-es) The Changing Woman Ceremony or the Gift of Changing Woman (the root of the word literally refers to stepping with one foot)

Ndee (in-deh) The people (the Apache name for themselves)